RACING ACE

Ride It!
Patch It!

Written by
Larry Dane Brimner

Illustrated by
Kaylani Juanita

ACORN™
SCHOLASTIC INC.

For artist Nancy Polster, a one of a kind, like Ace. —LDB

To all the bike riders who ring their bell before they pass,
and say hello when they do. —KJ

Library of Congress Cataloging-in-Publication Data
Names: Brimner, Larry Dane, author. | Juanita, Kaylani, illustrator.
Title: Ride it! Patch it! / written by Larry Dane Brimner ; illustrated by Kaylani Juanita.
Description: First edition. | New York: Acorn/Scholastic Inc., 2022. |
Series: Racing Ace; 3 | Audience: Ages 4–6. | Audience: Grades K–1. |
Summary: Ace gets her mountain bike ready for the big bike race, but
during the race Ace's bike chain comes off the sprocket, and a tire goes
flat—luckily she has her tools with her to fix the problem so she can finish the race.
Identifiers: LCCN 2021044958 (print) | ISBN 9781338553826 (paperback) |
ISBN 9781338553833 (library binding) |
Subjects: LCSH: Mountain bikes—Juvenile fiction. | Mountain
Biking—Juvenile fiction. | Bicycle racing—Juvenile fiction. | CYAC:
Mountain bikes—Fiction. | Mountain biking—Fiction. | Bicycle
racing—Fiction. | LCGFT: Picture books.
Classification: LCC PZ7.B767 Ri 2022 (print) |
DDC 813.54 (E)—dc23/eng/20211012
LC record available at https://lccn.loc.gov/2021044958

10 9 8 7 6 5 4 3 2 1   22 23 24 25 26

Printed in China   62

First edition, December 2022
Edited by Katie Carella
Book design by Maria Mercado

THE TRAIL

This is Ace.
She likes to race.

This is Ace's bike.

Ace washes the frame.

She makes her bike shine.

She cleans the spokes.

Ace gets her bike ready for the race.

She oils the chain.

She spins the wheels.

She tests the brakes.

Ace gets ready for the race, too.

She packs her backpack with tools.

She pulls on her gloves.

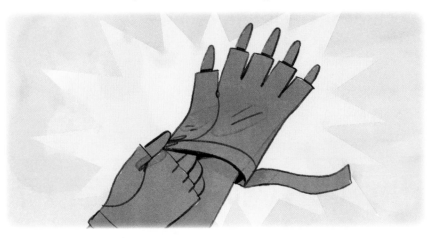

She snaps on her helmet.

Ace looks at the race map.
The trail ends where it begins.

There is a lot to remember, Ace.
Don't get lost.

Ace is almost ready for the big race. She must try out the trail first.

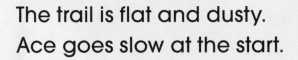

The trail is flat and dusty.
Ace goes slow at the start.

Then the trail swoops downhill.
Ace rides fast now.

Red dust swirls up behind her.
She rolls around a curve.

Look out, Ace!
She plops into the mud.

Mud flies everywhere!
It's good that you have a rag, Ace.

Ace pumps to get up the next hill.

Yikes, Ace! Rocks! Use the brakes.

The starting line is up ahead.

Now Ace needs her racing number.

Ace ties the number to her bike.
It's her lucky number.

Her helmet is in place.

Ace, you are ready to race.

SPEED AND DUST

Ace takes her place at the starting line. Other racers line up beside her.

Ace grips the bike's handlebars.

She puts one foot on the pedal.

The starter waves the flag.
Go, Ace! Go!

Racers speed down the trail.
Bikes kick up clouds of dust.

104

101

Ace holds on tight.

She pumps hard and fast.

Her feet spin in circles.

Come on, Ace. Go faster!

Ace passes one racer.

Then she passes another racer.

Ace pumps her legs up and down.
Oh no! Something is wrong.

Now her bike starts to go slower,

and slower,

and slower.

One racer flies by Ace.

Another racer zooms by her.

What is wrong, Ace?
She looks down at the spinning pedals.

The chain is off!

She rolls to the side of the trail.

Ace flips her bike upside down.

She fixes the chain.

Then she gets back in the race.

No, Ace! Not that way.

Ace spins her bike around.
She pops a wheelie.

Yes, Ace.
Now win this race!

OVER THE LINE

Ace races to catch up.
The other racers are ahead.

She zooms around the mud.

Now climb that hill, Ace.
She pumps hard. But she goes slow.

Uh-oh!

The back tire is going flat.

You know what to do, Ace.

Patch that tire.

Now pump it up.
It needs air!

There is no time to waste.
Finish the race, Ace.

She passes one racer.
Then the flag comes down.

Nice try, Ace!
You will win the next race.

ABOUT THE CREATORS

LARRY DANE BRIMNER

has never had to patch a tire on his mountain bike. But he has accidentally ridden through mud and had a loose bike chain slip off the sprocket. He lives and rides in Tucson, Arizona.

KAYLANI JUANITA

has never professionally raced a bike before, but she has ridden around a few neighborhoods. Her first bike was seafoam green with silver training wheels. Once the training wheels came off, she raced with other kids on bikes!

YOU CAN DRAW ACE!

1 Draw Ace's head and shoulders.

2 Add face details. Draw Ace's hair.

3 Add Ace's helmet and goggles.

4 Erase her head inside the helmet. Draw Ace's hands and the bike's handlebars.

5 Add Ace's eyebrows. Add the inside of her goggles.

6 Color in your drawing!

WHAT'S YOUR STORY?

Ace runs into problems during the bike race.
Imagine **you** join the race and run into problems.
What happens to your bike during the race?
Will you feel good even if you don't win a prize?
Write and draw your story!